Charlotte's Shadow

Anne-Marie DePape & Christine Quaglia

Tails Of
Charlotte & Shadow

This book is dedicated with love and thanks to all of our friends and family, to differently abled children and their families, and to furry friends everywhere.

Charlotte's Shadow

For more information:

Tails of Charlotte and Shadow
@tails_of_charlotte_and_shadow

ISBN: 978-1-7781643-0-9 (Paperback)

“Wake up Shadow. It’s morning!” says Charlotte. “Remember, wherever I go, you go. That’s why your name is Shadow.”

I hear Charlotte’s voice. Everyone calls her Charlotte but to me she is a real-life superhero.

My eyes open wide. I can hardly wait for today’s adventure!

POW!

S

Every morning I spring into action. I hurry to flick the light on in Charlotte's bedroom! Charlotte puts my vest on and says, "With this vest, I grant you all the powers of the Universe!"

Charlotte puts on her favourite sweater, tights and bracelets. As Charlotte puts on each item, she transforms into a real-life superhero!

Charlotte puts on her special goggles which I bring from her nightstand.

"Now I can see you!" she tells me while putting them on.

We go to the kitchen where Charlotte's Daddy says,
"Good morning! Are you ready for breakfast?"

"Always!" Charlotte replies.

"Here you go!" and hands Charlotte her toast and milk. "Power fuel for my little superhero." He then says, "Shadow, here's your favourite kibble."

Charlotte starts to play with the superhero figures she brings everywhere with her even the breakfast table. I hear, "POWWW, take that."

"Alright Charlotte," says her Mommy. "Let's put the superheros away until you're finished. Even superheros need their breakfast."

At the end of our favourite superhero cartoon show, Charlotte turns to me and says, “Shadow, are you ready for our adventure?”

I jump off the couch to get Charlotte’s backpack.

Charlotte’s Mommy says, “Now, don’t forget to visit Nana. Daddy and I also need this letter dropped in the mailbox, please.”

“We’re on it, Mommy!” replies Charlotte.

Charlotte puts the letter in my mouth and we begin our adventure.

We reach a busy street and Charlotte needs my help to get to the other side.

The light turns green and it's my time to shine! I lead the way across the street to make sure that it's safe for Charlotte.

We get to the other side and Charlotte says, "Good boy Shadow, we did it!"

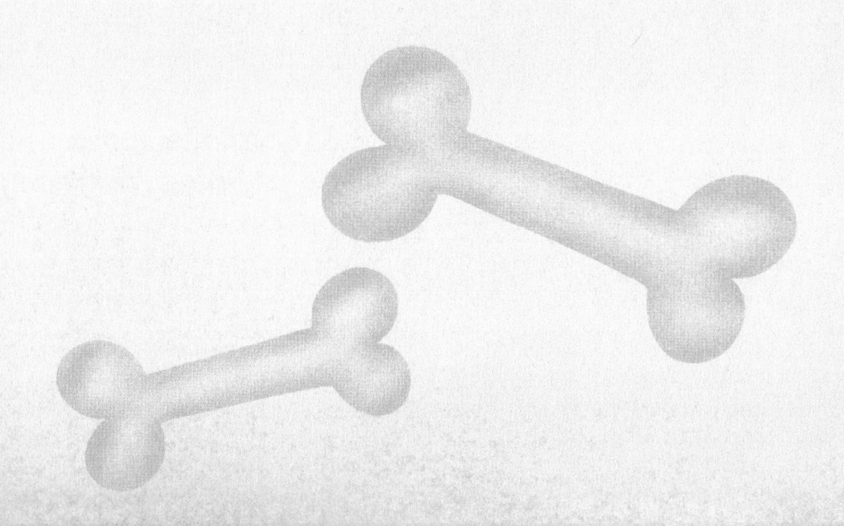

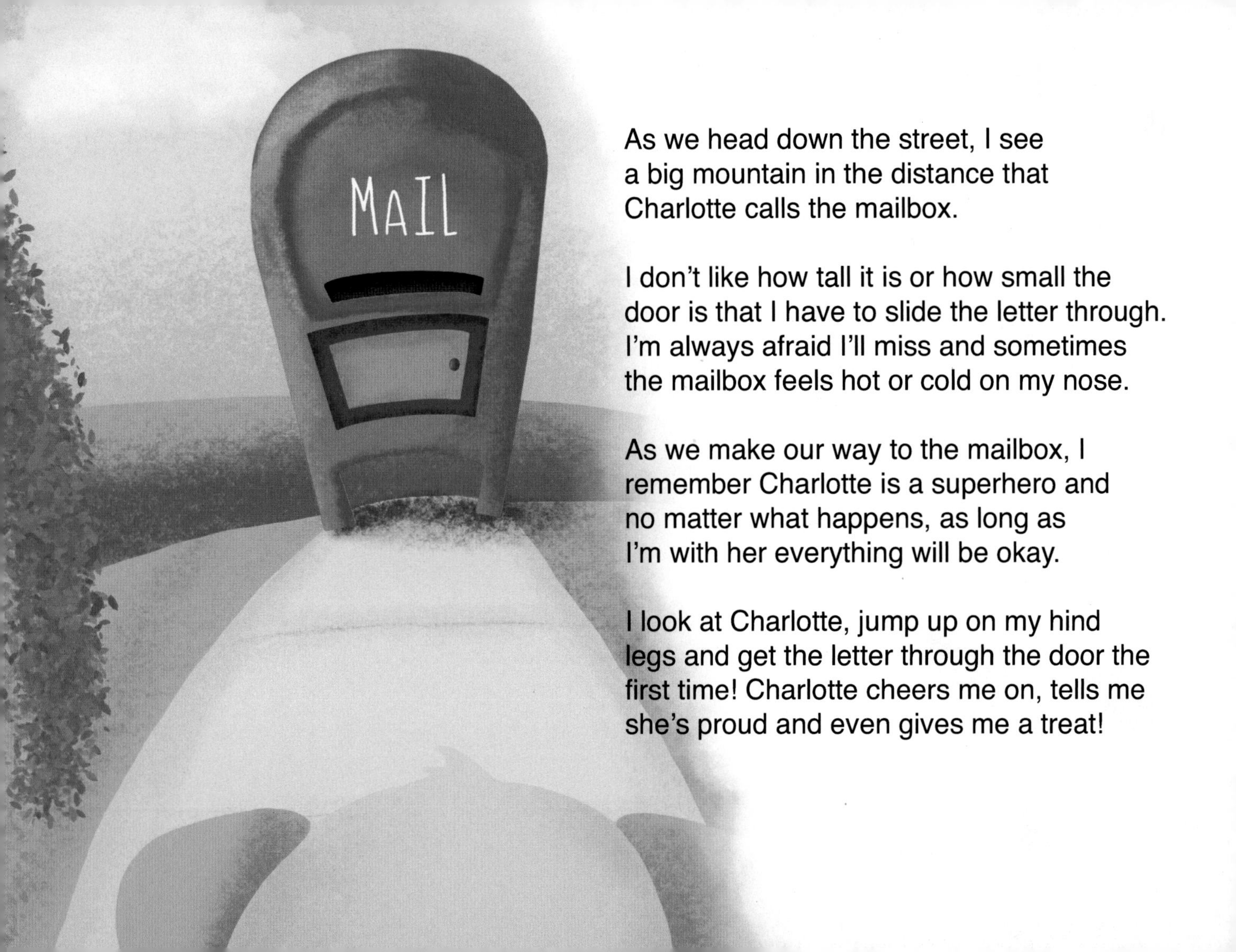

As we head down the street, I see
a big mountain in the distance that
Charlotte calls the mailbox.

I don't like how tall it is or how small the
door is that I have to slide the letter through.
I'm always afraid I'll miss and sometimes
the mailbox feels hot or cold on my nose.

As we make our way to the mailbox, I
remember Charlotte is a superhero and
no matter what happens, as long as
I'm with her everything will be okay.

I look at Charlotte, jump up on my hind
legs and get the letter through the door the
first time! Charlotte cheers me on, tells me
she's proud and even gives me a treat!

AIL

I always look forward to going to Nana's house. Her house smells delicious.

Nana is in her garden, waving and saying "Hello sweetheart! I've missed you!"

"I can really use your help watering. Can you please grab the watering can for me and help me water these flowers?" Charlotte says, "Fetch" and I bring the watering can to her.

Charlotte fills the can with water and moves it back and forth over the flowers.

After Charlotte finishes watering, Nana gives her a cupcake and gives me a special treat too!

Waving goodbye, Nana says, "Have fun at the library!"

As we get closer to the library, we see a boy near the front door
with his Mommy. I hear him say, “How come she gets to bring her
dog to the library and we had to leave Riley at home?”

His Mommy says, “Shhhh, Nathan” and doesn’t answer his question.

I think she’s embarrassed that they left Riley at home.
Maybe, they will remember to bring him next time.

LIBRARY

As we approach the big doors of the library, Charlotte says, “Open Shadow”
and I jump up and push a button, which opens the doors like magic!

“Well, hello Charlotte! How are you today?” asks Mrs.
Coulson who Charlotte calls a librarian.

“Fine, thank you Mrs. Coulson! I have a book to return” says Charlotte.

I fetch the book from Charlotte’s backpack and jump
up on my hind legs to put it on the desk.

“Thank you so much” says Mrs. Coulson. “Here Charlotte. This new book
came in but don’t tell anyone. I saved it just for you” she winks.

Charlotte thanks Mrs. Coulson and then we head to our usual spot
by the window to read. I love this spot because I can see outside
and there’s a vent right on the floor that fluffs my fur.

BOOK ReTURN

S

Nathan's Mommy tries to stop him but he comes over to Charlotte and says, "How come you can bring your dog here?"

"Shadow comes everywhere with me so he can help me. I'm in a wheelchair and Shadow helps me to do things that other kids can do on their own."

"That's so cool," Nathan says. "You're lucky. I wish my dog knew how to do those things! Can I pet your dog?" Nathan asks.

"No, I'm sorry, you can't pet Shadow because he's working and if you pet him that will distract him."

"Is that why Shadow is wearing a vest?" Nathan asks.

"Yes" Charlotte says. "Shadow's vest lets everyone know that he's working and shouldn't be disturbed."

"That's awesome!" Nathan says.

Nathan then waves goodbye to Charlotte and rejoins his Mommy.

LIBRARY

What an adventure we had today! We mailed a letter, crossed a street, watered flowers, read a book and even made a new friend.

I'm glad I can go on adventures with Charlotte everyday even to places where other dogs can't go.

I'm looking forward to tomorrow when Charlotte puts my vest on and says: "With this vest, I grant you all the powers of the Universe!"

I guess that makes us both superheroes.

I can't wait until our next adventure!

Tails Of
Charlotte & Shadow

Anne-Marie is a Developmental Psychologist, specializing in disability studies across the lifespan. Anne-Marie received her PhD from McMaster University and trained at world renowned institutions including the Max Planck Institute for Psycholinguistics in Nijmegen, Netherlands. Anne-Marie has worked in healthcare and education settings over the years, with her most recent position at Mohawk College where she is a full-time faculty member in the Department of Community Studies. Anne-Marie is passionate about creating early learning opportunities for children and enjoys spending time with her dog, Sammy.

Co-Author

Anne-Marie DePape

Christine is a full-time Social Worker and a part-time Writer. She loves to write about what affects all of our lives. Thoughts we have, questions we raise and the ways in which we can grow and, hopefully, come to know, and, to become better, so we can then do better. She obtained her undergraduate degrees in English and Psychology and her Master's degree in Social Work. She works at a Canadian university to accommodate students with disabilities. She has done a TedX talk on language and the perception of disability as well as written about her own personal experience of being born with a congenital neuromuscular disorder that requires her to use a wheelchair. She lives with Charlie the dog and both like being outside and taking long walks.

Co-Author

Christine Quaglia

Kenzie is a Graphic Gesigner from London, Ontario. She graduated from the Graphic Design program at Fanshawe College in April of 2022. Kenzie has had a passion for art from a young age which led her to her career in graphic design. She specializes in illustrative design and is very versatile with her drawing styles. She is passionate about bringing ideas to life through design and illustration, and enjoys time spent with her dog, Tags.

Illustrator

Kenzie Edge

Manufactured by Amazon.ca
Bolton, ON